Candler Mansfield

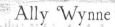

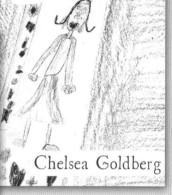

Chelsea Goldberg

Dianne Newberry

Elena Fenton

Ally Wynne

Written by Susan Johnston and Kimberly Webb

Illustrated by Maria Tonelli

This book is dedicated to our precious nieces and nephews:
John Owen, Va, Elena, Katie, Emily, Carly and Dillon

Wishing you all a Happily Ever After!

Thanks to all the young artists across the country who submitted their interpretation of Princess Bubble.

Princess Bubble, copyright © 2005
ISBN # 0-9650910-0-7
ISBN # 978-0-9650910-0-8

This book is published by Bubble Gum Press in the USA, 2006
Printed in China by Regal Printing
A percentage of proceeds will be donated to The Ronald McDonald House

Bubble Gum Press
P.O. Box 19535
Atlanta, GA 30325

Please visit us at www.PrincessBubble.com

nce upon a time there
was a beautiful and
blissful princess named
PRINCESS BUBBLE...

Princess Bubble graduated from the Royal University.
She then took a job for the Royal Heir Line. Ready for
adventure, the princess wanted to travel to other kingdoms
and lands. She wanted to meet new people and learn
about their cultures and differences.

Princess Bubble decided to buy a palace of her own,
and she decorated it with all princess decorations.
Other princesses loved to come to her palace
for dinners and movies! Throughout the land,
the other princesses gathered at her home for
all kinds of royal celebrations.

Several of Princess Bubble's friends,
Princess Twinkle, Princess Sparkle and
Princess Glitter, told Princess Bubble
they had found their princes!
These friends were soon to be married
with fancy, royal weddings.

Princess Bubble, Princess Swan and
many other princesses were asked to be
bridesmaids in their royal weddings.
They purchased long, colorful bridesmaids' dresses
and dyed satin shoes that they were told they
would wear again.

Princess Bubble hosted parties at her palace honoring the new brides. She bought lavish gifts for the princesses who were soon to wed and begin their "happily ever afters."

Married princesses frequently asked Princess Bubble,
"Why hasn't a beautiful princess like you found a prince?"
Princess Bubble did not know what to say.
She was happy! She was traveling, making friends and
helping others, but this princess was prince-less.

Suddenly, the queen called Princess
Bubble to the big castle on the hill
and said, "Princess Bubble, it is
now time for you to find a prince!"
The queen named many different princes from other
kingdoms; princes from good families,
like the Charming family, who had a young prince
and the Right family who had a young Mr.
Any of them would
make fine husbands.

TICK TOCK TICK TOCK

Princess Bubble decided that maybe the queen was right.
After all, that was how every fairy tale ended.
So she set out to find her prince!
She went to dinners, movies, parties, and football games
with many different princes and
thoroughly enjoyed them all!

She took the advice of her mom
and joined www.FindYourPrince.com.
With her mind in a fog, she even kissed a frog!
All the princeless princesses had long talks about
where their princes could be. But, Bubble did
not believe just any prince would bring her
"happily ever after."
Yet the fairy tales said she must
find HER prince!

So she put on her thinking crown
and re-read the fairy tales for clues
on where to find her prince.

She soon realized that unlike the other princesses,

She was not trapped in a dungeon...

She had no wicked
stepsisters or
stepmother...

She did not
know any
dwarfs...

Nor did
she
live
under
the sea.

But the most confusing
part was...

She was already happy!

Then Princess Bubble's Fairy Godmother appeared!

The Fairy Godmother told Princess Bubble,
"Living happily ever after is not
about finding a prince.
True happiness is found by loving God,
being kind to others, and being
comfortable with who you are already!
Happy princesses are people who
enjoy others and like themselves.
Happy people give of their time to help others."

Princess Bubble was shocked that all the fairy tales were wrong! Everything the Fairy Godmother said made perfect sense. She was already happy!

Princess Bubble loved her life, her family, and her friends.

Princess Bubble
    thought about all she
        had learned and looked
            forward to the many
            adventures ahead of her.

She knew she
would live
"happily ever after"...

...and
She
DID!

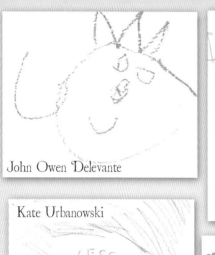

John Owen Delevante

Jacqueline McHale

Emma Delevante

Kate Urbanowski

The End

Kendall Mans...

Elizabeth Ellen
McKinney

Emily Fenton

Emily A
Cox

By: Sarah Stone

Princess

Sarah

Sarah Treadway

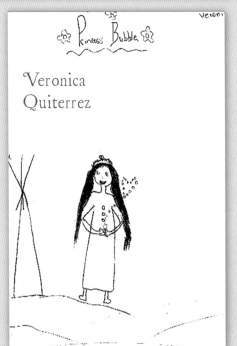

Princess Bubble

Veroni

Veronica
Quiterrez

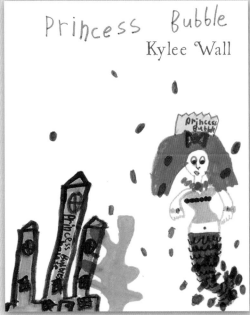

Princess Bubble
Kylee Wall

Princess Bubble